THE RELENTLESS ROGUE
A REGENCY STANDALONE NOVELLA

TRISHA FUENTES

ARDENT ARTIST BOOKS

The Relentless Rogue
Copyright © 2019-2024 by Trisha Fuentes
All rights reserved.

Book Cover and formatting provided by Trisha Fuentes
https://bit.ly/m/trishafuentes

No part of this book may be reproduced in any form or by any electronic or mechanical means, including information storage and retrieval systems, without written permission from the author, except for the use of brief quotations in a book review.

ISBN: 979-8-3302-2306-0 (Paperback)

Published by
Ardent Artist Books
www.ardentartistbooks.com

ABOUT ARDENT ARTIST BOOKS

Ardent Artist Books was established in 2008.

We publish modern and historical romances once a month!

For a complete list of our published books and books in development, please visit our website at:

https://ardentartistbooks.com/free-downloads

FREE DOWNLOAD
Updated Monthly!

Follow us on YouTube to see what new stories are on the horizon!

https://www.youtube.com/theardentartist

Like, Subscribe & Comment

LET'S CONNECT!

Fuel your love of fiction with exclusive content and captivating insights from Ardent Artist Books. Whether you crave the thrill of modern narratives or the timeless elegance of historical fiction, our newsletter delivers a curated selection straight to your inbox.

Plus, as a welcome gift, receive a FREE downloadable eBook:

"The Family Fix"

https://mailchi.mp/567874a61a56/aab-landing-page

THE RELENTLESS ROGUE

CHAPTER 1

BRIGHTON, 1800

Miss Selina Henning slowly slipped out of bed without Lord Harding noticing. The room was still dark enough for him to realize she was not lying beside him, but by this time surely, he did not care. She stood up naked, beside the bed and lowered her eyes down the length of *his* nakedness. He had been lying on his stomach, with his limbs exposed through the disarray of blankets on the bed. His hair was mussed from where she had run her fingers through it, he was muscular and lean and sun-kissed from swimming in the ocean.

They both had too much wine to drink that night, having met at a ball thrown for the Royal Family where he offered to give her a ride home. Instead, she arrived at his bachelor residence, through a secret entrance where he undoubtedly snuck in all his trysts.

She had to have him, at least once ... at least this is what she told herself when she allowed him to seduce her. His charm, his appeal, she knew of his sordid reputation, and she permitted him to have his way with her. He was a wonderful lover, and although she was a virgin when she allowed him to take her, she wasn't so now, and the thought of Lord Owen Rowley, the Earl of Trenton, her future husband, knowing she was no longer as innocent as she claimed, panicked her.

Selina tip-toed to her gown on the floor and picked it up along with her undergarments, shift, stockings and shoes and carefully walked over to a corner of his bed chamber to dress.

Lord Harding stirred in his sleep which caused her to pause, and she waited for him to fall back asleep so she could finish.

She'll always remember their kiss on the veranda under the moonlight. His heady breath was hypnotic and his lips divine. How one kiss could end like this was unfathomable she used to think, but knowing now the power he had over the softer sex, no others would be safe under his spell.

Finally fully dressed, she discreetly walked over one last time to gaze down at his lazy torso still asleep on the bed. His body was magnificent and she held high hopes that her future husband's would be the same. However, her fiancé was of medium height, unlike Lord Harding's tall stature, and she did love the fact that she was able to tilt her head up to kiss him.

She turned around and left the bedroom, and pulled her overcoat over her ball gown so that no one would notice her indiscretion.

"Pardon me," she heard a voice whisper as she descended the staircase, "I did not mean to alarm you."

Selina gazed down at Lord Harding's Butler and nodded her head, "You did for a moment," she whispered back, gathering her coat closer to her body. "I did not expect anyone in the household to be awake so early in the morning."

The Butler grinned and lowered his eyes, "I wake early when his lordship has guests for the evening."

Selina lowered her eyes, "Oh, I see."

The Butler cleared his throat before he voiced, "I have a cup of tea and biscuits ready for you if you would like, if not, I took the liberty of requesting his lordship's two-seater be ready at the back entrance."

Selina nodded her head and gazed beyond him, "The back entrance would suit me just fine, I thank you, Mister—"

"Cooper," he uttered with a bow.

Selina smiled at him and then stepped away from the staircase and proceeded towards the back entrance. She walked behind him as he escorted her towards the backdoor carriage ready with a single horse and driver. She quickly eyed Mr. Cooper and gazed into his eyes. "You are most kind Mr. Cooper, thank you for your hospitality and provision of my person."

Mr. Cooper bowed his head, "You are most welcome."

Selina took his elbow as she made her way into the carriage where he was about to close the door. "Am I to assume my driver knows my residency?"

Mr. Cooper nodded his head, yes, "Yes, Miss Henning."

Selina lowered her eyes again in modesty, "Thank you, Mr. Cooper."

"Miss Henning, is there a message you would like me to pass to Lord Harding?"

Selina watched Mr. Cooper close the door, and felt it finalized, "No, Mr. Cooper, no message."

Selina felt the tug of the carriage as it pulled forward, accomplishing her escape freely and without embarrassment. She gazed out the window and noted it was still dawn and was glad for it. She reached over and closed the window shut, she could breathe easier now, the awkwardness of the sunrise with Lord Harding would have been most uncomfortable considering. It was best that she left unseen, but she knew Mr. Cooper would be announcing her departure as soon as Harding awoke.

Luckily, she had been staying with relatives in Rottingdean, and would be able to sneak in from the rear of the main house. Her entrance would not cause concern or question and she could pass unnoticed when she arrived.

Closing her eyes at last, Selina instantly brought to mind Lord Harding's kiss in the moonlight. Measured and wonderful, his lips were soft, his tongue, vulgar in the way he tasted her deeply, over and over. How was she ever supposed to forget his touch on her skin? *She would not,* she concluded, reopening her eyes, for Lord Graham Harding would be challenging for any woman to forget, not just her.

CHAPTER 2

FIFTEEN YEARS LATER

*H*is Grace, the Duke of Whitehall, sprung from his bed and took a quick look down at the young miss still asleep. They had met at a garden party and he offered her a ride home in his coach. It did not take much for him to cajole his way for her to sit next to him on the bench. She was a lustful female most willing to be unpeeled.

He walked out of his bed chamber and into his private parlor where his Valet, Mr. Hemsworth had a bath waiting for him. Submerging himself in the warm water, the Duke stretched his legs out in his long tub he had especially made for two people.

The Duke eyed Mr. Hemsworth who was just about to leave, "Hemsworth," he voiced sternly, "send her away with one of the pre-made gowns in the dressing closet in the guest bedroom—the *pink* one. Do not allow her to linger till noon, have her out of here by mid-morning at best. Oh, and make sure the two-seater is available to take her home."

Mr. Hemsworth bowed and then voiced, "Yes, Your Grace, very well. Your coach will be ready by the time you are dressed, should I send Cooper up with some tea?"

The Duke nodded his head and grabbed the soap, "Yes, thank you Hemsworth." He waited until his Valet closed and locked the double doors behind him before he gazed down at the scar between his legs. *That dratted scar*, he thought, as he grabbed the soap and lathered himself up and down. Washing his chest and underarms he thought of what he had planned for today, and the many women he might meet. Blondes, brunettes', redheads, it did not matter, no female was out of danger if he were attracted to her. His charms were relentless in that the outcome would always be in his favor. But he was careful, always cautious not to flaunt his seduction of a lady out in public, but to secretly captivate her so that she would later give in.

Brighton was bursting with tourists, and many of them female companions of other females searching for adventure, and who better to fulfill those dreams? He almost never saw them again, and by morning they were either too embarrassed to chitchat, or gone without a further word. Some would sleep in his bed, escape by daylight and others would slip out in the middle of the night.

His bachelor residence was useful not only to his female guests but to himself with his ancestral summer home being thirty minutes away. His bachelor residence was a townhome just near the pier, and was a habitat not only serviceable, but convenient for his many trysts.

Lord Graham Harding, the Thirteenth Duke of Whitehall was tempting bait to any available female searching for a husband or male friendship. He did indeed have many female companions, all of which were familiar to him or simply not interested being devoted to their husbands. He enjoyed the company of many women, older, younger, and virginal—it did not matter for his one quest was never fully quenched, which caused him to repeat the pattern until the hallow in his heart would be filled.

Graham submerged his whole body under the water leaving his nose exposed for breathing. He thought about his past—then quickly his present—for times past were a painful reminder of how far he had overcome. He brought to mind only a handful of women who rarely experienced his true affection. More times than not, he was a cold-hearted predator who stole many hearts, and was never the least bit remorseful.

He sat back up within the tub and slicked back his dark brown hair allowing the drips of water to run down his cheeks, neck and shoulders. He would be attending a dinner party later that evening, for a friend of an acquaintance of a relative he just had been introduced to. It would be a small gathering of just twelve—some couples, and a few single accomplished ladies. He hoped one of them would succumb as he gazed down at his scar between his legs. *That dratted scar*, he thought, standing back up and getting out of the tub in a rage.

He walked over in just a towel around his midriff, and gazed down at the bed where the young miss was just thirty minutes before. He enjoyed her company, but now he must get on.

He thought about his past again, but quickly suppressed it for he could not allow his memories to haunt him today.

He walked over to his armoire naked, and opened up the cabinet to search for a clean shirt. The one he had worn previously was stained from the wine that tipped over when they made their way clumsily towards his bed.

Hemsworth appeared around the corner with his

shirt and pants and Graham immediately dropped his towel to the rug.

CHAPTER 3

The Duke sprung from his bed and then took a quick look down at the young miss still asleep. They had met at a dinner party and he offered her a ride home in his carriage, and without inhibition, the girl rushed to sit beside him and lunged for a kiss. *Who was he to refuse?* She was lovely, with lush pink lips, an ample bosom and she tasted divine.

He walked out of his bed chamber and into his private parlor where Hemsworth had a bath waiting for him. Submerging himself in the warm water, Graham stretched his legs out to the end of the long tub.

Graham eyed Hemsworth who was just about to leave, "Hemsworth," he voiced sternly, "send her away with one of the pre-made gowns in the dressing closet in the guest bedroom—the *blue* one. Do not allow her to linger till noon, have her out of here by mid-morning at best. Oh, and make sure the two-seater is available to take her home."

Mr. Hemsworth bowed and then voiced, "Yes, Your Grace, very well. Your coach will be ready by the time you are dressed, should I send Cooper up with some tea?"

Graham nodded his head and grabbed the soap, "Yes, thank you Hemsworth." He waited until his Valet closed and locked the double doors behind him before he gazed down at the scar between his legs. *That dratted scar,* he thought, resting his head back on the rim of the tub. Fifteen years back, his pelvis was trapped underneath a coach wheel that he volunteered to help fix. He fractured his pelvis that day along with severed pride for the surgeons all announced the same prognosis: he would be able to walk again, however, he would never be able to bear any children. He then took the soap and washed his penis and the remaining testicles he still had. Thank goodness he was still able to pleasure a woman for the thought of *that* would have sent him reeling into madness! He swished the water around with his hands and enjoyed the hot bath on his back and legs. Immediately, his thoughts recalled the past evening. She was the daughter of a guest of his solicitor. From the moment he spotted her, he knew he had to have her. Her brown locks and bright blue eyes consumed him throughout the evening as well as her full bosom. She was intelligent, animated and constantly challenged him during their game of whist, and he loved the way she threw her head back in laughter at one of his witty remarks. All night he imagined throwing her head back in rapture, and she did not disappoint when he finally won the chance to root her.

He would be seeing his mother today, along with his brother, his wife and their three children. His father passed five years ago, which left him peerage and inheritance with provisions. On his father's death bed, he had his will rewritten for Graham to inherit all property and annual income on one condition; he marry. His father knew of the severity of his possible impairment, but still required Graham to at least try and father a child. *Bastards were welcome,* he remembered his father telling him. Bastards were the living breathing reminder of one's presence and vitality, but Graham should at least try ... and attack, he did.

He had become known around Brighton has a scandalous rake with the worst reputation. Seducing females every chance he received to test out his father's theory, young, old, widowed or married; no one was protected. Lingering inside them, hoping that his efforts bore fruit, but none ever did, and a few years later, all he cared about now was finding himself a wife so that he could keep his inheritance.

Graham swished his hands underneath the water and watched his penis grow and swell. He must have been thinking about his conquest of the past evening, how he had her several times then sprung to his feet to see if he could take her again before she left.

Walking over to a peep hole he had specifically created to learn whether his companions for the evening left or not, Graham was surprised to see his bed, vacant.

He walked out of the parlor and over to his armoire naked, and opened up the cabinet to search for a clean shirt. The one he had worn previously was torn from the exercise he spent with the avid miss, and the lewd festivities they both shared.

He would have to seduce another, he thought quickly, closing his armoire door. Perhaps at his mother's tea party he would find another prey. A friend of his mother's, a daughter of a close friend it did not matter, as long as the female was willing, she would be in his bed.

"LADIES AND GENTLEMEN, MY SON, HIS GRACE, the Thirteenth Duke of Whitehall," the Widow Harding announced to all her guests. She had been hosting a tea party for no particular reason other than a cure for boredom, and searched for company far and wide. Newly arrived from London, her guests were impressed by Whitehall Manor with its lawns and gardens overlooking the seaside and ocean beyond. Their manor was built cliffside, two hundred years prior, and remained their ancestral home in Brighton. Every summer, they enjoyed countless parties, guests from France, Spain, India and anywhere else seeking a cure for their ailments.

Most of her guests came from London, and other cities to cure their aches and other diseases. In the middle of the Eighteen Century, doctors began to claim that diseases could be cured by bathing in sea-water. King George III was the first monarch to believe this advice, and he regularly visited Weymouth for a swim. His son, the future George IV, spent a great deal of time in Brighton, and eventually built the Royal Pavilion in town.

Rich people tended to imitate the behavior of the royal family, and holidays by the sea became very fashionable. The number of people visiting these resorts increased further because of the claims made by some doctors that drinking sea-water would cure asthma, cancer, consumption, deafness and rheumatism as well, resulting in the Widow Harding having plenty of companionship.

The Widow Harding arrived alongside her son who had been planted by the fruit trays plucking grapes off their stems, "Your Grace, come with me to my parlor for a moment, there is something I wish to discuss with you."

Graham gazed beyond at their party, and their many guests sitting at the tables enjoying themselves on the lawns underneath their white tent. "Sure mother," he voiced, pin-pointing his brother Alex, sitting down eating with his three boys.

Graham and his mother arrived in her private parlor, and he watched her close the double doors behind her. Leaning up against the wood, she stared at him for a few seconds then ambled in to take her seat. "I have asked you here for purely selfish reasons," she voiced, smoothing down her skirts while seated.

Graham took a seat across from her, and casually crossed his legs so that his boot lie flat on his thigh, "Why else? You are not in the custom of inviting me to one of your parties where the softer sex is in abundance."

The Widow Harding grinned at his cleverness, "Or did I?"

Graham smiled at her humor, "Missed you mother. I am elated to see you are well and in good spirits."

The Widow Harding tilted her head, and lowered her eyes down the length of her eldest son. *He was put together very nicely,* she often thought. Who would have known that a tall, lean Gentleman like her son would afford such attention with his dark brown hair and hazel eyes? Stares from her friends, daughters of her Gentlemen acquaintances, no female was safe. She figured he received all of his good looks from his father, for he too was considered handsome. "How is the hunt, my dear?"

Graham let go a roguish grin for he knew what she meant, and it did not involve a fox, horses or spaniels. "I met someone last evening," he mentioned, sort of matter-of-factly, "polished girl, accomplished, well-versed, and witty."

"Is she from good family?" She asked, sipping her cup of tea she had her housemaid's bring in before their conference.

"Henning," he nonchalantly expressed, standing back up to serve himself a cup as well, "In from Northampton and staying with relatives in Rottingdean."

CHAPTER 4

"Henning?" She questioned, gazing out the window. "Your father had a business associate once named Henning, is it perhaps his acquaintance? They have interest in the Royal Pavilion I hear."

Graham bit down on a biscuit then gazed out at the ocean blue. His heart beat escalated at the thought of what might be on the horizon. "The very one," he replied, chewing and sipping his tea, "Miss Henning mentioned her family interest in the Pavilion, they must be one and the same."

The Widow Harding was glad to see that her son was at last interested in courtship, "Your father's will."

Exasperated by the darn thing, Graham stood up abruptly and walked away from his mother, "What about it? Is there some new provision I did not know about in previous discussions? Am I to acquire a monkey or elephant perhaps in addition to a wife?"

The Widow Harding laughed out loud, "No, my dear, but you are coming dangerously close to its timetable. Just a few more months and you will lose everything to your brother, Alex."

Graham closed his eyes in that moment, *father a child in the next few months? What madness was this?* He had been attempting breeding at every waking moment, with no results from his lascivious merits, how was he supposed to accomplish this simple task? "Then what are you proposing, mother? Do I take a chance with one of your house guests today? Miss Wedsworth perhaps? Or possibly Mrs. Banfield? I hear in certain unseemly circles that she has already accepted her son's best friend."

His mother raised her eyebrow, "Is she now? No wonder the woman looks remarkably fresher these days."

Graham smiled but did not gaze her way. "Should I extend an invitation to the Henning's? Invite their family to one of your many garden parties?"

"Good idea," she voiced, shaking her head in agreement. "Next Wednesday," she expressed, standing back up to her feet. "Next Wednesday, I have nothing planned. I will make the arrangements while you go call on the girl."

"You mean *now*?" Graham voiced, rankled.

"The sooner the better," she demanded, keeping her stance.

Graham closed his eyes again, "I do not call on the softer sex."

"Then change your character, son," she quipped, "time is of the essence."

Graham let go a huge sigh.

Rottingdean

GRAHAM HAD HIS DRIVER STOP JUST OUTSIDE the gates to the country house where Miss Martha Henning had been staying with relatives. This courtship business was a bothersome nuisance to say the least, he had not recalled the last time he did court a female ... *when was that? Oh, that's correct ... never.*

He looked across at its simpleness and rolled his eyes. *His future wife would have no dowry,* he presumed, but then thought quickly, *it should not matter.*

He made his way through their tall grasses and wildflowers, and headed for the front door. Hesitating for a moment, he gazed around him and recalled their ocean view. He had been there before ... years prior ... it felt like another lifetime. *Was Miss Henning related? He simply must find out.* He knocked on the door a few times and waited until it opened.

"Yes?" The man asked, "May I help you?"

"The Duke of Whitehall to see Miss Martha Henning, is she in?" Graham asked, holding his hat in his hands.

The man paused and looked him up and down, "Why yes, she is, Your Grace. Come inside, while I go and announce you."

"Thank you, sir," he uttered as he walked through the door. The inside was humble, but clean and well kept and the man asked him to wait in the side parlor as he headed out a door. Graham ambled over to some photographs up on a mantle over their large hearth. Black and white photos of children, elders and one of a wedding. He focused on one in particular but then did a double-take to see Miss Henning framed by the door.

"I am very surprised to see you Your Grace," she curtseyed, then walked into the parlor.

Graham dropped his eyes down the length of her, she appeared different in simple cotton, "I was on my way to Newhaven and I was wondering if you would like to accompany me?"

Miss Henning gave him a small smile, "I will get my gloves, coat and bonnet."

Graham nodded his head at her choice, "I shall wait outside."

Martha Henning was elated and let out a small scream as she ran up the staircase to her room. Their country house was owned by her cousin, the widow Rowley and held several rooms on the upper floors and just a few with a kitchen downstairs. The servants all stayed in the cottage in the rear, while the family resided inside in the main house.

Martha ran into one of the rooms still excited and startled her second cousin half to death.

"What is it?" Lady Elizabeth asked, placing her reading book in her lap.

"The man of my dreams is in our front yard!" Martha squealed towards the window, "Waiting on me to grab my coat, gloves and bonnet!"

Lady Elizabeth Rowley, the thirteen year-old daughter of the Widow Rowley came running to the window, "Let me see!"

Martha bit down on her lower lip and pointed at the glass, "See how handsome he is!"

Elizabeth's eyes grew wide and surveyed the man with his hat atop his head, "I cannot tell from this view. Can we ask him to turn around, or at least look up?"

Martha pinched her cousin's shoulder and then quickly yanked her coat out of the dresser closet and snatched her gloves and bonnet, "I must hurry! I must get on!"

"Bye Martha!" Elizabeth smiled, running after her and then freezing at the sight of her mother coming out of her room.

"What is this noise?" Her mother asked, gazing down the staircase and seeing the blur of skirts descending.

"A Gentleman called on Martha!" Elizabeth screeched, running back towards her bedroom window.

Curious, her mother walked after her and over to the window herself. Surprised to see Martha being offered the Gentlemen's hand and into his elegant carriage. She wondered about it for a few seconds more, and then walked away without a care.

CHAPTER 5

Inside the carriage, Martha could not contain her joy. The mystery was solved, for now she knew that the Duke's sinful ways were best attributed to how many times he could make her welp from climax. She lowered her eyes down the length of him, and received that same jolt of passion from the other night, the one where she threw herself across the carriage and into his open arms. She contemplated doing it again, but she did not know where they were headed, and did not want to be discovered having intercourse out in the open air. "Thank you for the gown, Your Grace," she voiced low, with a tease in her timbre. "However did you know my favorite color?"

Graham gazed towards her now sitting across from him inside his coach interior, "Blue matches the color of your eyes," he relayed, equalling her gutter tone and lowering his eyes to her blue gown. He brought his eyes up to her frame and became somewhat puzzled. Seeing her in daylight quite startled him. He did not realize or fathom the many freckles she had across her nose and cheeks. Her eyes, he did remember, but the sun's rays were now enhancing the gold in her brown hair. "Your family, Miss Henning," he relayed quickly, "your father Mr. Hubert Henning?"

Martha's eyes lit up, "No, Your Grace, Mr. Hubert Henning is my Uncle, my father is Mr. Howard Henning, they are twin brothers. Should I come sit by you?"

Graham shifted in his seat, *he would like that very much*, but too many carriages were passing by them ... they might be discovered ... however, the danger of being unveiled was quite tempting. "Not yet, Miss Henning," he relented, gazing out the coach window. "Your family, Miss Henning, tell me more about them."

Martha looked at him oddly and then her heart leaped for joy. Inquiring about one's family could only mean one thing—*engagement*! "The Henning's derived out of Northampton, *Sir*. Both brothers are employed by the same construction company which aided in building the Royal Pavilion. There are talks of expansion, which my father and Uncle are very excited about."

"Oh, I see," Graham said, nodding his head, "That is

where my father met Mr. Hubert Henning, at a ball for the Royal Family when they were here last in Brighton."

"When was that?" Martha asked, curious. "I do not recall a ball for the Royal Family."

"About fifteen years ago, I believe," Graham let go, assured about the time. "Your mother?"

Martha let go a huge smile, "From Northampton as well. Grew up with my cousins, we are a very close family."

Graham smiled, "I have one brother," he proclaimed out loud. "And we are *not* close at all."

Martha's smile dropped, "How very sad," she relayed, eyeing the hills disappearing all at once, "my family come together at least four times a year. One being the summer months, we all travel to Brighton to enjoy the cool weather."

"How old are you?" He laughed, dropping his eyes to her bosom by mistake.

Martha grinned at his flirtation, "Twenty-seven Your Grace, and old enough."

"Any siblings?" He asked, his smile dropping down to a thin line. His heart began to escalate with the possibilities of the conversation.

"An only child, but I did grow up with my cousins," Martha uttered, noting that the Duke looked disinterested. "My favorite cousin was fortunate to marry the Earl of Trenton."

And there it was.

Graham's affirmation of familiarity, and he now turned to fully look her way. He knew Lord Owen Rowley, the Earl of Trenton very well, they both attended Oxford when they were younger and he was saddened to hear of his untimely passing. "So sorry for your loss," he softly expressed, lowering his eyes. "I knew him when we were younger, we both graduated from Oxford."

Martha now lowered her head, "Yes, we were all shocked by his death. He was a good man," she said, melancholy, "most generous and loving to his wife and two children."

Graham scratched his head and desperately wanted to clear out of this uncomfortable conversation. *Loving to his wife, she said, and their two children?* His past arrived to the present like a lightening bolt. He became noticeably awkward being too close to Miss Henning, and acted like a cougar trapped in a cage. "My mother would like to invite you and the Henning family to Whitehall Manor next Wednesday."

Martha thought it odd how strangely he asked, "We would be delighted to join you Your Grace, please extend our thanks and gratitude for the invitation from the Widow Harding."

"You're most welcome," he quickly spat out, not looking her way. Just then, Graham felt incredibly ill. Just the thought of being married made him sick to his stomach. He did not want to marry Miss Henning, in fact, he did not wish to marry anyone at all! If it weren't for the provision in his father's will, then he would not have to contemplate *any* union. His brother and his three boys were now in the lead, and Graham would soon have to step down and watch his hateful brother move into his family manor, and take over *his* annual income. *Why was this happening? What purpose did it serve? His father knew of his sterility upon his death, why force him to father a child or find a wife when he knew very well he could never have them! Why not just hand over his peerage to his younger brother with three boys on his death bed? They would be inheriting upon his own death, so why not just give over the property and peerage outright?*

CHAPTER 6

"Where is your mother?" Martha asked Elizabeth, pacing back and forth watching for any sign of a carriage drawing near.

"I told you already," Lady Elizabeth remarked, gazing up from her book in her lap. "She went into town."

"But that was *hours* ago," Martha whined, pulling back the curtains and taking another look. "She should have been home by now."

"Where were we invited Wednesday?" Lord Duncan Rowley, the fifteen year-old son of the Widow Rowley asked, sitting next to his sister with his limbs crossed.

Martha did not look back at her second cousins, and continued to gaze out the window, "Whitehall Manor in Brighton. I hear that the Widow Harding throws some of the best picnics out on her lawns."

"I do like picnics," Duncan smiled, snatching the book out of his sister's hands and reading the title, "*Mansfield Park* again? Read *Waverley* by Sir Walter Scott."

Elizabeth reached over and grabbed the book back out of her pestering brother's hand, "I rather like Jane Austen thank you very much, and prefer to read *Mansfield Park* twice, than anything by Sir Walter Scott."

"Here she is!" Martha shouted, startling the two bickering siblings. Martha picked up her skirts, and ran to the door to greet her cousin. "Oh do hurry—hurry in, there is something I must tell you!" She yelled out in front of her waving her cousin inside.

The Widow Rowley tried to catch her bearings, "What has happened? What news?"

Martha smiled graciously, and waited for her cousin to take off her bonnet and gloves before spurting out, "We have been invited to Whitehall Manor for a picnic on Wednesday!"

The Widow Rowley stared at her cousin oddly, "What?"

Martha jumped up and down with joy, "The Widow Harding has personally invited the Henning family to Whitehall for a picnic! And," she said, gazing around at her curious second cousins, "I believe the Duke is about to propose!"

"To whom?" Duncan asked, honestly.

"To *me*, silly!" Martha squealed, clapping her hands.

Elizabeth stood up and shrieked along with her. Running to her side she gave Martha a hug, "Oh, how romantic!"

Martha gave the girl another squeeze and rested eyes on her cousin who seemed frozen in thought. "Selina?" She asked, releasing Elizabeth and stepping into her. "The color has escaped your face ... you all right?"

Lady Selina Rowley, formally *Henning*, never thought this day would come. Brighton was a large enough city for her to get lost in with its many tourists and regular natives, and Northampton was almost a world away, and not once had she crossed paths with him ... *not once* ... until *now*. Now she was invited to his very doorstep and expected to see him again? *And, what is this? Her beloved cousin Martha, soon to be engaged to the Duke of Whitehall?* Selina turned around to find a chair to sit down in. She wiped her brow off with the back of her hand, and gazed across at her loving children. Elizabeth, so sweet, learning to play piano and becoming an accomplished lady and her son, almost sixteen, such a fine, young man who absolutely adored her since the passing of her husband. She hated her husband and was glad he was dead, for now she was free to live her life without being cautious. *Oh, how did this happen?* Hearing the Harding name again, she could feel her heart beat faster. Closing her eyes, she brought forth her cherished memory of lying naked in his bed. Limbs entwined with his, caressing his backside after entering her for the third or fourth time. His lips, so soft and inviting, his caresses—his touch! "I shall decline," she whispered, meekly.

"What dear?" Martha asked, rubbing her cousin's shoulder. "Did you just say you are declining?"

Elizabeth sprung to her feet, "What? But how will I ever meet new friends?"

Duncan too, stood up tall on his two feet, "I was hoping to join a hunting party or maybe could ask His Grace to join his."

Selina slowly closed her eyes, it was of no use. There would be a time and a place for everything, and her time seemed to be now. *She could avoid him, she could, make sure she was not in his vicinity or peripheral view. She could hide out at the picnic all day and go sight unseen, that could work, could it not?* She raised her eyes and then asked, "Has anyone bothered to ask your Grandfather or Uncle their opinion about attending this picnic?"

Martha shrugged her shoulders, she knew her father was a hard sell and did not warm to social gatherings, "No, not yet. I wanted you on board first, then I can speak to my father."

Selina gazed down at her shoes, she knew this picnic might just be the end of her. "Fine," she quickly said, standing back up to her feet. "But do not ask me to play any games."

Martha grabbed her cousin and gave her a warm hug, "Oh cousin, thank you! Thank you—now I shall have a talk with my father."

Selina smiled at Martha as she spun around in search of her Uncle. She then gazed down at her two children, "Now, you two."

"Can I purchase a new dress? New ribbons for my hair?" Elizabeth asked her mother, excited all of a sudden.

Selina nodded her head, yes. "Of course you may, my darling, and you Duncan? What is your request?"

Duncan stood up and stepped into his mother. He grabbed her hand and kissed the back of it, "To see you happy, Mum … just to see you happy."

CHAPTER 7

BRIGHTON

WHITEHALL MANOR GARDEN PARTY

*I*t took her nearly half the morning to get ready, having changed her dress so many times. This one too colorful, that one too dull, none of them acceptable which made her settle on a long gray-green skirt, and a dark green Spencer jacket. She pulled up her golden hair in a simple coiffure which was hidden underneath her cotton and straw lawn hat.

Martha was just the opposite, and dressed a bit too elegantly for daytime with her silk and ruffles, and Selina hoped it did not rain.

On the carriage ride over, Selina had never been more nervous. Her father and Uncle both jumped at the chance of conversing with some of the Widow Harding's regular guests in attendance and rented a separate carriage.

Selina wanted to sit in the coach for the remainder of the garden party the moment they arrived through their gates. Whitehall Manor was a gorgeous country home with manicured lawns, rose gardens and water sculptures. They were asked to walk around the manor to a rounded gate where it was easier to access the rear yard and where the picnic was being held.

The moment she eyed all the many guests, Selina's heart calmed down. She could get lost in this crowd, *so many*, with thirty, maybe fifty people in attendance. The Harding picnic was merely an outdoor ball by the looks of it, with guests drinking, eating, playing lawn games, some even dancing to a string quartet in the far corner. There were even several chairs spread out to sit along the cliffside, to enjoy the ambiance and view of the hills and ocean beyond.

Selina gazed over at her children who were in awe of the general splendor and she guided them forward as they made their way towards the Widow Harding and her family to be introduced.

And there he was...

Standing beside his mother, while his younger brother, Alex, his wife and their children positioned last.

His Grace, the Thirteenth Duke of Whitehall stood tall, erect ... and unsmiling? He appeared different to her then before. It had been nearly sixteen years and the young buck had matured into a handsome stag. He was twenty on that night under the moonlight when she had him, back then he played with his boyish charm, she could only imagine what charisma he owned now, at thirty-five.

"Widow Harding," she heard her Uncle announce, "how nice it is to see you again."

The Widow Harding lowered her eyes and acknowledged the fine looking Gentleman, "Mr. Henning, it has been quite awhile, has it not? What—ten, eleven years?"

"More like fifteen," Howard corrected her, smiling. "May I introduce my family, my brother, Mr. Hubert Henning, his daughter, Lady Rowley, her children, Lady Elizabeth and Lord Duncan Rowley, and *my* lovely daughter, Miss Martha Henning."

"Nice to meet you all," the Widow Harding smiled, "there is plenty of entertainment for everyone, food, drink, amusement ... and your wives?"

"Passed on, Madam," Howard pronounced, bowing his head, "terrible accident ten years ago, both my wife and my sister-by-law drowned off the coast of France on a passage back to Portsmouth."

"Oh, how awful," the Widow Harding relayed, gazing over at her son, staring at *Miss Henning … or was it Lady Rowley? She couldn't figure out whom …* "My son, the Duke of Whitehall, my youngest, Lord Alex Harding, Lady Harding and my grandsons, Stuart, Henry and Christopher."

Selina smiled then curtseyed along with her cousin Martha and children. She looked up unexpectedly and felt her heart drop to the pit of her stomach. Every inch of her screamed not to look his way but she did it anyway and their eyes locked and held. Dark hair, graying at the temples, a fuller face with a romanesque nose, his eyes, heavenly hazel and—*oh God!* She wanted to *run*, she wanted to *hide* but there was nowhere she could duck away to!

Graham's eyes followed along the Henning party, and bounced from one jovial personality to the next, until his eyes rested on … *her*. Mr. Henning announced *Lady Rowley, so she did marry him after all?* Her golden locks and warm brown eyes took his very breath away, she was older yes, but a beautiful mature female. His eyes tore apart from her for a moment only to be drawn back to her like a magnet. *Finally,* he thought instantly. *Finally his past came back to the present.*

"Your Grace?"

Graham immediately snapped out of his haze and looked down at his mother, "Yes?"

"Mr. Henning asked you a question, dear," the Widow Harding relayed.

"My apologies," he said quickly, eyeing the man, "can you repeat the question?"

"Is that a billiards table outside, Your Grace?" Hubert asked next, pointing to a game already in progress.

"Do you play, Mr. Henning?" Graham asked, curious.

"Why yes," Hubert replied, walking away from the women with the Duke, "played two or three games a week while in London, I daresay, I am pretty good."

Graham grinned at his sudden competitor, "Then we shall have a match, you and I."

"I would like that very well," Hubert agreed, nodding his head, "very well, indeed."

CHAPTER 8

"I know her," Elizabeth pointed out, "may I go sit with Miss Cluett, Mum?"

"There's a few friends of mine over there as well," Duncan pronounced, walking away and bowing his head.

Selina gave her daughter a small smile. "Sure, and I will be," she said, gazing around the area, "... over there." *Over there* really meant out of sight of the Duke, and Selina opted to sit on one of the chairs overlooking the sea. It was peaceful there, the sun was shining bright with a cool breeze that swept up from the hillside. Selina was starting to rest easy until she spotted the Duke walking straight for her.

She was just about to make a mad dash towards the refreshment table when she saw her cousin Martha corral him in mid-trek.

"Are you avoiding me?" Martha asked, wide-eyed and flirtatious.

Graham lowered his eyes to hers once then looked back up again to see Lady Rowley disappeared from her seated position. "No," he quickly said, grabbing her hand and placing it on his elbow. "Are you enjoying yourself?"

"I wasn't before," Martha teased, "but I am now if you must know."

Graham let go a grin and in the corner of his eye, he spotted Lady Rowley by the candied jellies, "Miss Henning, there is someone I must speak to," he voiced, sternly, "meet me at the buffet in about twenty minutes, we shall enjoy a meal together."

Martha nodded her head and released her grip on his forearm, "Promise?"

Graham lowered his eyes to her ruffles and open bodice by mistake, "Promise." He did not look back and walked away from Miss Henning in search of the enchantress in forest green. Lady Rowley had been by the sweets just a few moments ago, but then she vanished again. *Why does she do that?*

Selina finally found an area where she would not be recognized, behind some full manicured hedges where a bench had been conveniently placed. From her vantage point, she could distinguish her daughter laughing with two other girls and her son, talking in a circle with his friends hundreds of yards away. She could also smell the ocean nearby and placed her candied jelly down beside her and closed her eyes to take in the sea breeze. She would never get tired of smelling the salty ocean air, if she had it her way, she would live in Brighton permanently. Selina reopened her eyes to see the Duke standing before her.

"I did not mean to frighten you," Graham voiced softly, immediately noting Lady Rowley's bizarre look.

Selina shook her head. "I did not expect anyone to find me here," she relayed, eyeing the tall foliage surrounding her and then back at him.

Graham stepped into her but still kept his distance, her presence was making his heart beat faster and he could not fathom why. "It has been many years, Lady Rowley."

Selina lowered her eyes, "Yes it has, Your Grace."

Graham dropped his eyes down the length of her, she was a vision in green, "My condolences to your family."

"Thank you, Your Grace," Selina voiced, feeling her throat close up.

"Lord Rowley and I were good friends when we were lads."

Selina lifted her head and bore into his eyes, "I know."

Graham wanted to know so much more and mostly *why?* He did not realize how much he missed speaking with her until now, but he did not wish to appear too anxious. "I did not know your family came here in the summer months," he said, lowering his eyes. If he had known, he would have made a visit to her sooner.

Selina gazed away from his overwhelming presence, "Yes, the Henning's make the trip two times a year to Rottingdean."

Something was amiss. Words that should have been spoken were not, and he cleared his throat before he asked, "You reside currently in Northampton?"

Selina closed her eyes and lowered her head. She wanted to know more about him too, but did not wish to appear too anxious. She did not realize how much she missed speaking to him until now, the feeling to be by his side was exciting she did have to admit. It was all too much too soon and she stood up abruptly, "Pardon me, Your Grace, I must return to my party."

Graham watched her as she ambled towards another direction, her head held low as she traipsed away on the grass holding her hat in place so it would not blow away. She had not changed much. Her brown eyes sparkling in the sunlight, her fair complexion and supple skin. The feeling to be by her side was overwhelming he did have to admit. He would have to corner her again before the day ended, this much he knew for sure.

THE WIDOW HARDING SAT BACK IN HER LAWN chair and admired the elder Henning Gentlemen playing billiards with some of her other guests and Mr. Hubert Henning's grandson. She appreciated the thinness of Hubert's build, his graying hair and strong arms. He appeared athletic, refined and was so intriguing she could not tear her eyes apart from him. It had been quite awhile since she was attracted to another man. After her husband passed, she went into deep mourning, and prohibited anyone from calling her formally *Her Grace* or *Dowager*. When being introduced she always insisted on being called the *Widow Harding*, it was a shield she wore well, and protected herself against the wolves who would be after her substantial wealth. But with Mr. Hubert Henning, she would gladly allow *him* to see her silk undergarments if he were to dare ask.

She gradually surveyed all the men surrounding him and picked apart each one and knew for certain her allurement to Mr. Hubert Henning. Then her eyes bounced from him to the next, only to rest on his grandson. An irregular curiosity surrounded the boy, as she sipped her wine and nibbled on a biscuit. She knew his father well, Lord Rowley used to come spend the summers with Graham, and the two boys liked to swim in the ocean and hunt for rocks for their collections for school. *Owen's son looked nothing like him,* she recollected, discerning that Owen was rather short in stance, with strawberry-red hair and a blanched complexion. This boy was tall in stature, and approaching full maturity for someone his young age, his hair was dark brown, his skin, tawny from the sun, and there was something about him that seemed oddly familiar.

Then she gazed over at his sister, who seemed shorter than her older brother with beautiful strawberry-blonde locks. The Widow Harding turned back and nearly choked on her biscuit, when Mr. Henning told a joke and the boy laughed. *His smile ...* the way he closed his eyes and gazed down at the ground ... was the way her eldest son smiled while closing *his* eyes to gaze down at the ground. He was the epitome of Graham when he was growing up. *Were her eyes deceiving her? Was it the sun on her face? The sea breezes floating up from the hillside that were playing tricks with her eyes? Was it the wine?*

CHAPTER 9

ROTTINGDEAN

*T*hank goodness her cousin Martha monopolized the remaining time the Duke had the rest of the afternoon. Selina did not have to bother with bumping into him unexpectedly again, her cousin had him tied up with all sorts of activities: shuttlecock, card games, even a long walk out towards the cliffside.

Selina woke up with the rain pounding on the rooftops, happy that the clouds did not roll in until today, otherwise the Whitehall picnic would have been a disaster.

She rolled over on her side and watched the water stream down her paned windows. She closed her eyes and instantly brought to mind the event of the day before. Her children were pleasantly happy, conversing and laughing with their friends, enjoying the sun and weather and *she* ... was unhappy, dodging the Duke at every turn and angle. It was almost like a game by the time they had left, pretending to forget something, her satchel, her hat and running towards their carriage and already sitting down in its interior once her party arrived.

She knew it was rude not to say goodbye to the hosts but she did not want to risk having to speak to him again.

Then there was Martha ... *dear Martha*, her beloved cherished cousin. Ten years apart, she used to watch the baby for her Aunt and when she died suddenly, Selina almost felt like her older sibling and took care of her. If courtship was what the Duke was trying to accomplish by inviting the Henning family to Whitehall, then he succeeded very well in that her Uncle would be made aware soon of his intentions. If an engagement entailed, then Selina would have to somehow fit His Grace in with *her* family. *Oh what a tangled mess,* she thought, rolling over on her back. Staring up at the ceiling she could hear the rustling and bustling of her children in their rooms. One most likely was reading a book, while the other was probably getting dressed to go outside in the rain in search of frogs. But which one was which?

Selina was just about to pop out of bed when she heard a knock on her door. "Yes?"

"Selina?" Martha asked, on the other side, continuing to knock. "It's me Selina, may I come in?"

"Come in Martha," Selina said, setting her back up against her pillows. "What is it? What's happened?"

Martha came in and shut the door behind her. Sitting on the edge of her cousin's bed she showed Selina a note, "This came early this morning."

Selina lowered her eyes and then brought them back up again, "Who from?"

Martha clutched the note inside her hands, "From the Duke of Whitehall. He wishes to call on me this afternoon."

Selina tilted her head, her cousin did not appear to be as cheery as the other day when the Duke came to call, "And? Why are you torn? Did he make an inappropriate advance on you?"

Martha was about to reply and tell her cousin the truth that the Duke *already* advanced on her several times in one night, but decided against it. "No," she said softly, "I have second thoughts."

Selina looked at her cousin oddly, "Why? What happened? What has changed your mind?"

Martha began playing with the rim of her skirt, "The Duke of Whitehall is a terrible rogue. Every maiden knows of his shameful reputation. Should I consider him a faithful husband? Should I take that risk? He will be wanting to speak to Papa soon, I just know he will be asking for my hand."

Selina shut her eyes and then reopened them, "And this does not make you happy, why?"

Martha shook her head and gazed out at the rain, "Yesterday, at the picnic, I was introduced to Mr. John Cahill from Wood Green. When he spoke, I could not tear my eyes away, his voice was like syrup to my very ears."

Selina was shocked by her declaration, "Are you smitten by Mr. Cahill?"

Martha shook her head, yes. "Oh yes," she cried, quickly, "and I believe he with me! Later, before we left, he asked to call on me today as well. I said yes, without hesitation and without thinking of the Duke or his intentions. Oh Selina dearest, what do I do? With two Gentleman callers in one day? I will look to others as a trollop!"

Selina whipped the bed covers apart from her legs, and swung them around and walked towards her robe that had been hanging over a chair. "No one will consider you a trollop Martha, just a very fortunate girl."

Martha turned to look at her cousin and with wide,

tearful eyes she asked, "Will you speak on my behalf and send the Duke away? Will you make an excuse for me?"

Selina shut her eyes again and sighed, "Must I?"

Martha then got up from the side of the bed and ran to her cousins side, "Oh please Selina, I beg of you! The Duke of Whitehall is not the sort of man who takes no for an answer."

Selina wondered what she meant by her tone, "Why me? Why not my Uncle?"

Martha grabbed at her robe, "Because I do not want to give His Grace the chance to have a private conversation with Papa, that is why."

Selina rolled her eyes and gazed out at the rain one last time. Maybe the Duke of Whitehall would not make the trip, knowing that the roads would be dangerous, and his carriage might get stuck in the mud. *Hopefully he would be sending his apology very soon.* Selina sighed, "I will speak to him on your behalf."

Martha wrapped her arms around her cousin and gave her a big squeeze, "Oh thank you! Thank you Selina, thank you!"

Selina smiled down at her and kissed her forehead, "That is what family is for."

CHAPTER 10

Selina's heart dropped when she heard his carriage pull up. The rain had not stopped since the morning and she was sure that the roads were already marshy and not fit for driving. Mr. John Cahill would be making the trip as well as her father and Uncle who left early into town, *wasn't anyone careful these days?*

"The Duke of Whitehall for Miss Henning," their footman announced, sending Martha in a panic.

"Oh no!" She shrieked, gathering up her sewing and throwing it into a basket near her seat. "He is *early*, and Mr. Cahill should be here at any moment as well! What do I do?"

Selina stood up and smoothed down her skirts, "Go into the other room, Martha. I shall speak to him on your behalf. You are sure you do not choose him?"

Martha did not hesitate, "No dearest—am I mad? Preferring Mr. Cahill over the Thirteenth Duke of Whitehall?"

Selina was relieved for some odd reason. In her own heart it injured her to know that the Duke had designs for her cousin and her cousin's interest in him. "No dear," she replied to Martha then looked over at her footman, "Chester, please show His Grace into my father's study. I will meet him there in a moment."

"Very well your ladyship," he said, with a bow.

Selina stepped over to Martha and held her shoulders, "Stop panicking, the Duke will not know of your other caller, I assure you."

Martha gave her cousin a hug, "Oh thank you Selina." She then let her go, picked up her skirts and walked away to hide.

Selina turned towards the door and hesitated for a moment. She would be face to face with him now, there would be no huge party to hide away in, or tall hedge bush or carriage whisking her away. She would be entering into the lion's den.

Selina opened up the parlor door and walked down the hall towards her father's study. It was really a combined office with two desks so that the brother's could work side by side without having to yell across the span.

Selina walked in and stood motionless, the Duke had been standing by the study's large full window and the blue in his jacket enhanced his good looks. "Thank you for waiting, Your Grace."

Graham held his hat in his hands and played with the rim. He did not expect to see Lady Rowley, and yet, it was why he made the arduous journey to the Henning country house in the rain. Twice they had to stop on the road to clear the mud from the carriage wheels, his driver's even insisted they go back. No, nothing would stop him from speaking to her today, nothing. After that debacle at the picnic, he knew of the urgency. Her face haunted him nightly, and he simply could not get her out of his head. "Lady Rowley, so nice to see you again," he remarked, tipping his head.

"Do sit down," she said next, feeling her throat close up.

Graham gazed down at the chair but did not take a seat, he fathomed what her presence there meant, "No need to express Miss Henning's refusal, Lady Rowley, it is you I am here to call upon."

Selina's heart dropped in that moment, for the way he said it sent shivers down her spine. His brooding stare, his roguish grin, *how dare him affect her body this way!* "Your Grace, I—"

"At the picnic the other day," he spoke up

interrupting her, "your constant disappearance was whimsical I do admit. Infected me in a way where I thought of nothing but to be by your side." He then placed down his hat, and stepped over to her still standing by the doorway. She had not moved an inch. Looking down at her peering up at him, "Later that evening I realized why."

Selina slowly closed her eyes and bit down on her lower lip, stepping away from his closeness she let go, "It was a mistake, Your Grace, all those years ago, a foolish girl who made an impulsive decision."

Graham lowered his eyes down the length of her and recalled that night nearly sixteen years ago. *He was a young buck and fearless after bedding two of his housemaids which gave him the courage to approach Miss Selina Henning when he spotted her at the ball. The Royal Family invited everyone who had been involved in the making of the Royal Pavilion, and the Henning Brothers and their construction company were one of the guests in attendance, along with their wives and family. Martha would have been eight or nine at the time, and would have not been permitted, but Miss Selina Henning having come-out at seventeen, was. Lord Owen Rowley was his best friend, a childhood mate, and Graham knew of his recent proposal to the Henning maiden and Graham was simply curious what his best buddy found so fascinating about her. From the moment he asked her to dance however, he knew what captivated him. He was relentless in his pursuit of her attention that night, he does remember that, and often times flirting with her in front of Lord Rowley. She was divine, with her golden brown hair, and elegant posture in her pale red silk ball gown. His allure to her was foreign however, having never been so engrossed with his housemaids before.*

Selina swallowed hard and tore away from his eyes in that moment. Perspiration was beginning to form on her forehead and she was sure he would begin to notice it. She walked over to the window and recalled that night at the ball. *She was engaged to Lord Rowley, he had proposed to her just that week, and it was a small celebration of sorts for them to be seen together out in public. She was in love with him, so she thought ... until her eyes crashed into Lord Graham Harding's. Owen always spoke about the heir to Whitehall, but she had never met him before that night. He was mesmerizing, tall, fashionable and relentless in his sordid attention. When Owen turned his head, the Duke of Whitehall would leer down at her; when Owen left for refreshments, the Duke would pull them into a darkened corner just to be next to her. There was no way out, but to give in. Then without warning, a messenger came for Owen, his mother was ill and she sent for him. Owen had to leave the ball but insisted Selina stay to enjoy the once in a lifetime activities of the night with the Royal Family in attendance. The Duke assured his best friend that he would look after her ... and he did. Whisking her away to the veranda, stealing a kiss from her in the moonlight; one kiss was just not enough, and the two of them hopped in his carriage and away to his bachelor residence he had in town.*

Selina reopened her eyes, and was startled to see the Duke standing next to her.

Graham took her hand in his, and brought it up to his lips, "You remember that night?"

Selina nodded her head and gazed into his eyes, "I do."

Graham lowered her hand but remained holding it, "I often thought about you, if you were happy with him." He hesitated, then bore into her eyes and whispered, "Were you happy with him?"

Selina did not wish to lie but she did it anyway, "Very happy, Your Grace."

Hearing her declaration injured him physically, and he turned around abruptly to grab at his hat. "But you gave yourself freely to *me*," he voiced sternly.

Selina could tell he was irritated for some reason, "Yes, Your Grace and an error in my good judgment."

"Why did you turn me away the next day when I called upon you?" Graham asked, watching Selina's eyes go wide with shock.

"The next day?" She asked, swallowing her pride.

"To this very house," he remarked remembering everything now, and circling his eyes around the room. "I was sent away."

CHAPTER 11

Selina gazed out the window, and noticed another carriage pulling up. Distressed, she hurried towards the door to open it. "You must leave at once," she let go, uncaring at how it appeared.

Graham studied her stance, and then turned his head towards the window, "Why? Who is here?"

Selina rolled her eyes, *she was not cut out for this sort of nonsense!* "Another caller for Miss Henning if you must know."

Graham laughed out loud, "And you thought I would be insulted?"

Selina opened the door wider, "Yes—but by your flippancy I may have been mistaken."

Graham leered down at her, she had deliberately ignored his previous questioning. He did not want to be forced to leave, not without an explanation. "Will you have dinner with me?"

Selina opened her mouth wide and then closed it shut, "No."

"Why not?" Graham teased, "Are you worried about your reputation my dear? What if I told you that we would be alone with no prying eyes or others to worry about? Whitehall Manor at seven, I will send a carriage."

Selina's heart began to pound. Every inch of her screamed to run away again, but heard herself say, "Yes, Your Grace—now go."

Graham gave her a roguish grin before setting his hat atop his head, turning down the hallway, he spotted Miss Martha Henning, and Mr. Cahill in the sitting room conversing. "Good day Miss Henning, Mr. Cahill," and then left.

"Why do I need to leave?"

Graham gazed down at his mother sitting in her favorite chair. "I did ask nicely."

"But why dear?"

Suddenly exasperated with her curiosity he blurted out, "Because I have asked someone here to dine, and I would rather this particular guest not be seen at my bachelor residence in town. There, happy now?"

The Widow Harding stood up and then circled her son, he seemed abnormal to her these past few days, like a persistent hiccup bothering her throughout the day. "Miss Henning I presume? Are we to expect an announcement soon? Did you speak to her father?"

Graham closed his eyes and then reopened them. "No mother," he plainly uttered, "*not* Miss Henning. Miss Henning has set her cap for Mr. Cahill."

"Did she now?" The Widow Harding acted surprised. "Nonsensical girl, choosing untitled gentry to a sixteenth century peerage?"

Graham walked over to a glass decanter of brandy and poured himself a drink. He was no longer interested in Miss Henning but her older cousin, Lady Rowley. *How did he get himself into this disarray?* "I have invited Lady Rowley to dine this evening ... *alone*, mother."

The Widow Harding stopped in her tracks and swallowed her smile. How many nights had she tossed and turned over a possible secret kept from her son? *Too many,* she thought as she was about to exit. "A widow?"

Graham raised his eyes towards hers, "Yes, mother."

"Honorable," she said, under her breath, "most honorable."

Selina dressed for the occasion but her mind was elsewhere. Inside she was dying and somehow could not stop the momentum of their drawing power. She contemplated not attending but her cousin talked her into it. Martha, for some odd reason, pushed her towards him, and gave her blessing to catch him if she could. Selina did not want to entrap anyone, much less the Duke of Whitehall. She wanted to close that door on him forever!

Selina sat in her coach and contemplated on what to do next. She asked her driver to give her a moment until she could discover her breath. She gazed out of the carriage window several times, but could not muster up the courage to step down.

Up above on the second floor, Graham watched as her black coach arrived around the bend. He stood immobile as the coach lingered and let no one down. He speculated on its inhabitants having second thoughts, and watched in dread when he saw her horses nudge forward.

Graham did not hesitate, and ran out of the room and traipsed down the staircase only to run down the hallway, and out the front door. The coach was barely at the front gates when he sprung forward, and continued to run after it. Finally gaining the driver's attention, the coach stopped, and Graham went to the door and flung it open.

Out of breath, he stepped up into the coach interior and plopped himself down on the bench across from her. Calming himself down, he straightened up his waistcoat and jacket then necktie, "Leaving so soon? When you have not yet finished the first course?"

Selina choked back her tears. Every inch of her was exploding with chance after chance but she was stubborn enough to ignore them. "I am not feeling well, Your Grace."

Graham dropped his eyes down the length of her, she was stiff in her seated position but looked well enough by the rose in her cheeks, "I shall have my cook make you some broth."

Selina dropped her eyes to his red waistcoat, "No, I must leave."

Graham tilted his head and soaked in her anguish. She had been squirming in her seat and he doubted why. "Just once allow me to take care of you," he whispered, feeling a lump in his throat. Unbelievable the sentiment that unexpectedly came out of his mouth, and as soon as he said them, he wished he had not.

Selina gazed into his eyes and allowed a single tear to

drop down one of her cheeks. "We shared one night Your Grace, do not assume you know all of me."

Graham drowned in her sorrow and simply could not take any more of her pain, "No—Lady Rowley, I do not assume, but I am assured you are in anguish and it distresses me to see you in such pain."

Just then, Selina doubled over and burst into tears. With her gloved hands to her face, she ruptured on the coach bench.

Seeing her fall over, Graham knelt on the floor and grabbed her body into his so that she could continue crying on his shoulder. He hugged her body close and felt her arms wrap around his backside and neck, burying her face in the crux of his shoulder. Continuing to blubber within his confine, he carefully set her back on the bench but held her body close so that she could let loose her heartache. Caressing her hair and shoulders, he leaned in and gave her a small kiss on her forehead. "By now, you and I are familiar," he whispered to her by her ear, "there are no false pretenses between us, we have already shared more than most men and women ... if anything, Selina, I am your friend, now and always."

CHAPTER 12

Selina pushed his warm comforting body away from hers, "I do not want your friendship!"

Graham shook his head and yanked out his handkerchief from within his waistcoat, "Here then, take this and blow your nose."

Selina gabbed the handkerchief away from him and dabbed at the sides of her nostrils. "You do not know me," she whimpered freely, "you do not know the depth of my pain."

Graham reached for her shoulder, "No, I do not assume to know the depth of your suffering, but I am willing to listen."

Selina sat back up straight and shook her head, "No, I cannot."

Graham stared out in front of him, nighttime was

already upon them, "Here then, let us fill our stomachs with supper. It will be some time before you make it back to Rottingdean."

Selina turned to look at him again, he too was afflicted with some sort of inner torment, "Your Grace, I sent you away that day because Lord Rowley found out about us."

Graham immediately stiffened and then turned towards her, "Found out—*how*? He left to service his ill mother."

"But waiting for me at my home the following morning," she sniffled and dabbed at her eyes. "I confessed and told him everything, but he still chose to marry me."

Graham shook his head and ran his fingers through his hair, standing up, he took her hand and led her out of the carriage, walking side by side out in the open air, they began to confess yesteryear, "But Lord Rowley did not say a word. Did not confront me, *nothing* and allowed me to walk untouched throughout the entire wedding party."

"He demanded distance between us and severed all ties with Whitehall," she said, blowing her nose.

Graham shook his head and ambled on, "Yes, I often wondered why his letters completely stopped or came back unopened."

"He was a good father," Selina continued, walking the lawns and garden now. It appeared romantic in the moonlight with the fire lamps all around them. "But a vengeful husband," she expressed softly.

Graham halted, and twirled her body around so that she could face him, "Unforgiving, how?"

Selina wanted to continue to suppress her torment but felt as if he needed to know. She bit down on her lower lip, "He would call me hurtful names, ridicule me in private, push me to the ground … kick me, throw jewelry at me, *anything* to show his frustration with what happened between us."

Graham shook his head, he could not believe what he was hearing, gathering her up within his arms, he voiced, "My eternal apologies Lady Rowley, it was never my intention to ruin you further."

Selina was beside herself. Being so close to him, within his arms again was her ultimate doom. *There was no way out, but to give in.* She deliberately tilted her head up to his and slowly allowed herself to lean in towards his mouth to taste his lips. Slow, careful kisses quickly turned to frenzied zeal, and the two grabbed at one another like magnets.

Feverish with passion, Graham only knew of one place where no one would find them and he picked her body up within his arms and swiftly brought her to the atrium.

Completely dark inside, Selina began to unravel his necktie desiring to buss his bare skin. Graham brought their bodies down onto a patch of grass inside the atrium and assembled hers over his so she would not get dirty. Straddling his torso, she leaned over him and continued to kiss his lips with open mouth grazes that suddenly turned erotic and deep. Graham reached down and unbuttoned his pantaloons while Selina pulled up her skirts and yanked off her undergarments. Simultaneously, Selina pushed into his hips and yelped at him entering, thickset and smooth as she rocked on his torso continuing to kiss him. It had been too long since she had any physical contact on her skin and the sensitivity of a man deep inside her, she relished in the two extremes, feeling him draw down her bodice and discharging her bosoms to his mouth and tongue, licking, suckling and kneading sending her to euphoria and climax. He clamped down on her hips and held her there to release his.

It had happened so fast, with no time to think, out of breath, she dropped on top of him and allowed what came about to sink in. With the dizziness of passion still lingering, Selina got up on her knees and then to her feet only to wobble towards a bench. She tried to fathom him in the darkness but then felt him suddenly sitting down next to her.

"My apologies Lady Rowley, passion overcame me," Graham softly voiced.

"Mine too," Selina whispered, closing her eyes, "There is no need for apologies, Your Grace, it was what I wanted as well."

Then silence.

A deafening silence.

"You're not going to run away again, are you?" She heard him whisper next.

Selina swallowed her smile. "No, I enjoyed my time here, but I must get on," she whispered back, reaching for his chin and kissing his nose.

Graham leaned in and gathered her face within his hands. Kissing her lightly, he inquired, "If I call on you tomorrow, will you send me away?"

Selina closed her eyes, "Give it a few days? Allow the fairy dust to settle?"

Graham let go a roguish grin, he knew exactly what she meant, "A few days then, and nothing more."

CHAPTER 13

Selina sat down on the sand and watched the waves roll in and out with the tide. It had been a few days since bedding the Duke again and she needed time to think.

Strange, how her body reacted to his so quickly, and how his hands on her skin became greedy and wanting more. She had forgotten what it was like to be intimate with another man, Owen had stopped touching her years before his death. He grew sour and blatantly flaunted his mistresses; she recalled waiting up hours throughout the night, hoping he would not come home intoxicated or angry enough to hurt her.

She wanted to divorce him but felt guilty for having bed another man just before their nuptials. Years of trying to make it up to him turned rancid and worse. It was true what she said to the Duke of Whitehall, that she was surprised that Owen did want to still marry her. But what she did not tell His Grace was how her father increased her dowry to solidify the offer. His Grace was not made aware that the Rowley family was in debt and that his best friend was nearly penniless. That the only thing Owen could offer her was his title, a small manor in Northampton and an acre of land.

To save on expenses, her father, Uncle and cousin, Martha all moved into the small manor occupying every available space along with her two children. Combining their incomes together, everyone had a better chance at survival than strenuously trying to make it on their own. The attic was turned into three extra bedrooms with a small parlor thanks to the brother's construction company. The house servants were built separate quarters off the manor, with each of them given their own rooms and a service kitchen.

Selina would be leaving Rottingdean soon, with the summer months ending in a fortnight. Packing up their trunks and shutting down until the weather turned again—oh how she wished time would slow down.

She dug her bare feet into the sand and relished in its warm comfort on her toes. She would be leaving, *yes …* and leaving *him* behind … for a second time. *She was in love with him,* she thought, closing her eyes and allowing the sunshine to bear down on her cheeks. In love with him again ... *had she always been?* Realizing the truth right then and there, tears swarmed her eyes. She grabbed the rim of her skirt and wiped away her torment. She was just about to bury her head in her knees to have a good cry, when she heard a woman's voice ring behind her.

"Quite a trek coming down that hill," the Widow Harding remarked, catching her breath.

Selina was shocked to see her with an umbrella in her hand which she used to brace her trail. She quickly found her feet and curtseyed, "Your Grace, how did you find me?"

The Widow Harding turned to look back up the hill she just came down from, "Your house servant mentioned you were by the ocean," she replied, gazing out towards the sea. "Remarkable how the blue can comfort one's woes."

Selina let go a small smile, "May I walk you back to the cottage?"

"No," she quickly replied, opening up her umbrella to shelter her face from the sun's rays. "There is something I would like to ask you."

Selina looked at the Widow Harding more closely. She wasn't more than twenty years older than herself and was still attractive. She was thin, unlike most of the women her age with graying hair around her temples and above her eyebrows. She owned the same eyes and nose as the Duke and Selina could not help but beam because her own son inherited those from *her*. "Yes, Your Grace?"

The Widow Harding gazed out at the ocean and cleared her throat, "My dear, you have besotted my son. I have never seen him in such pain."

Selina blinked back her impact, "I must confess that your son does entertain the softer sex."

"Do not be coy with me, Lady Rowley," she said, with disdain, "I do not have time for imprudence."

Selina gulped and then looked across at some seagulls flying through the air, "There is no indiscretion Your Grace, I speak the truth about your son."

"What about the truth?" She snapped back, boring into her eyes. "How many years have you kept the truth from my son?"

A fear spread through to her skin and her heart sunk. *What was she speaking about? The night she slept with her son the first time? How did she know?* "Pardon?"

"Do not stand there and appear dumbfounded, Lady Rowley," she replied, discouraged, "you have been harboring a secret for many years now."

Selina slowly closed her eyes and brought her fingers up to her nose to pinch it, she felt a headache coming on … "You are mistaken, Madam."

The Widow Harding shook her head at her, "Your eldest is the living, breathing illustration of *my* eldest, there is no inaccuracy there."

Selina lifted her head high ... *There was no way out, but to give in.* "He is his son," she said through a cracked voice. "But the Duke of Whitehall does not know."

"You must tell him," the Widow Harding rejoined promptly, "for my son has a confession for *you*."

CHAPTER 14

Selina could not help but feel it was a trap. She would be walking into heartache, she could feel as much in her bones. She left the Widow Harding that day with nothing more but questions and had avoided confronting the Duke till this day; the day they were to leave Rottingdean for Northampton.

Their trunks packed, the cottage furnishings covered and the home, sealed. They were just about to head off down the hill towards the main thoroughfare, when their coach and party were obstructed by the Whitehall carriage on the road.

Martha gazed out of the window and noticed the Duke walking towards her father and Uncle sitting on the wagon full of trunks and personal belongings. "Oh no!" She exclaimed, in a panic, "The Duke of Whitehall is here to cause havoc, I presume."

Selina closed her eyes, she could only imagine what her father must be thinking, "Are you sure it is him?"

Martha gazed out the window again, "Know him anywhere."

Elizabeth leaned over as well, "Let me see," she asked, peeking out the other side. "Oh how handsome he is!"

Duncan peered out the window as well, "What is he doing here?"

Selina just shook her head. She had avoided him since that day she spoke to his mother, she could only assume he was there for Duncan. A pit was felt in her stomach, as she could hear her father conversing with the Duke.

"I apologize for the intrusion, Mr. Henning," Graham said, getting out of his own coach. "But I ask for a private audience with Lady Rowley, it is of the upmost importance," he replied swiftly, "I promise I will take her to the crossroads where we will meet you to drop her off."

Hubert turned to look at his brother. Howard lifted his eyebrows in agreement and Hubert turned back towards the Duke. *Whatever it was, it seemed important.* "We will meet you at the crossroads, Your Grace."

Graham nodded his head and then walked over to the coach where Lady Rowley and her family were all in attendance. Opening up the door he was surprised to see all four of them seated, with surprised looks pasted to their faces. "Lady Rowley," he asked with a bow, "may I escort you to the crossroads?"

Martha, Elizabeth and Duncan all look her way. Selina's heart was felt in her throat, she gazed at her daughter first then replied, "If my children do not object."

Elizabeth smiled at her mother, "I will be fine, Mum, do not worry."

Selina then rested her eyes on her son. In her peripheral view she could see his father and indeed, the two were identical. She reached out to touch Duncan's face, "See you at the crossroads."

Duncan nodded his head, yes.

Selina then reached down and accepted the Duke's hand as he helped her down the steps and walked her over to his coach. With all eyes still upon them, she reached into the interior and sat down.

Once inside, Selina felt the carriage tug forward as his driver turned the vehicle around to point towards their destination.

She sat across from him in silence and doubt. His mother confessed that the Duke had been besotted, *could this be the reason he has come after her? What a tangled mess,* she thought gazing out the window and watching Rottingdean pass her by. *How could she leave him now?*

Graham sat across from her in silence and doubt. *Why was she leaving without at least sending him a farewell?* A letter, a messenger with a note, anything would have sufficed, instead she remained a mystery and it tormented him to no end. He cleared his throat before saying, "We seem to be two ships that pass in the night."

Selina grinned at his diverting comment, "With no compass or stars to guide us."

Graham let go a small laugh, "We are no longer children you and I, and have maintained friendship, until *now*."

Selina could tell he was upset, he kept rubbing his hands up and down his thighs, "Surely, Your Grace you are used to females leaving before dawn."

Graham lowered his eyes down the length of her, she had been twisting her hands on her lap and was nervous for some reason, "Very much so."

"I *had* to leave," Selina softly voiced.

Graham sat back casually in his seat, "Why? May I ask?"

She turned her head to swallow her tears, "It was a mistake, the other night."

Graham shifted in his seat, "The other night, fifteen years ago—all mistakes? Yet, you seem to be willing to make them."

Selina was about to get up but he beat her to it and tugged at her skirts to sit her back down. "If you wanted to trap me here to insult me, then release me at once."

Graham let go a huge sigh and shook his head, no. "Not until I liberate something I have held on for many years."

He held on? Selina could not believe her ears! It was of no use, everything that was felt, everything that had come to pass was better left unsaid. "Then you will release me to my own carriage?"

"Yes," he quickly admitted, watching her eyes fill with sorrow. He then took his hat from the seat next to him and began fingering the rim, "Fifteen years ago, on my way back from Rottingdean on that day you refused to see me, I volunteered to help fix a passing coach who's wheel had come off. While trying to help holding it in place, the other broke which caused the entire carriage to tumble down on top of me, trapping my hips and legs underneath."

Selina sat in awe and disbelief. She sent him away because Owen had been there with her! Brow beating her to confess her misdeeds and to hold her to their engagement! Her heart *hurt* in that moment, *what would have happened to them if only she would have seen him when he came to call?* She covered her mouth up with her gloved hand, "Oh Graham."

Graham laid his hat down beside him again and bore into her eyes, "I fractured my pelvis that day along with severed pride for the surgeons all announced the same prognosis: being able to walk would be imminent, however, I will never be able to bear any children."

CHAPTER 15

*T*ears swarmed her eyes all at once when she fathomed all the missteps that were taken just to get to this point. She took the handkerchief away from his hand and dabbed her eyes, "I sent you away because Lord Rowley had been there with me … threatening to ruin my reputation, and forcing me to marry him."

Graham could not believe what he was hearing! *All those years of wondering what if? Where would they be if she had only come to the door?* She had bewitched him the previous night, overtook his senses and forced him to come to resolution. *She* was who he wanted to marry all along! No other woman would suffice. Bedding one after the other, it was no wonder Miss Martha Henning came extremely close! Miss Henning was just a surrogate for her cousin—Lady Selina Henning Rowley! In that very moment he fathomed how much he loved and adored her, and would not be able to breathe from this day forward. "Selina," he carefully said, stepping over and sitting down on the empty spot beside her. He took her hand in his, "I'm in love with you, I just realized I may have always been. I do not want you to go back to Northampton, but to stay in Brighton, and marry me. Will you do me the honor of accepting my hand?"

Selina dabbed at her eyes again and felt her heart burst wide open. *All those years of wondering what if? Where would they be if she had only come to the door?* He had captivated her the previous night, overtook her senses and forced her to come to resolution. *The Duke of Whitehall* was who she wanted to marry all along! Not Owen, never Lord Rowley! "Yes," she blurted out, grabbing at his shoulders and crying in them, "I will marry you."

Graham was happy at last and any doubt that remained, vanished. Holding her body near, he kissed her on her bare shoulder, then her neck before looking into her eyes, "Today? Will you marry me today?"

Selina had never been more sure, "Yes, Graham, today. But first we must stop my family before we make it to the crossroads."

Graham gazed outside and noticed familiar territory, "We are already here at the crossroads."

"We are?" Selina asked surprised, looking out the other window. They were and felt the driver and the horses slowing down.

"Today?" The Widow Harding asked, astonished. "You will not give me a week to prepare? Throw a lavish party with an ice sculpture, or musicians?"

They were all back at Whitehall Manor, standing, sitting in their grand parlor overlooking the ocean beyond. The brothers were side by side, while Miss Martha and Lady Elizabeth were seated. Lord Duncan Rowley was by himself, standing just behind his sister while Selina and Graham stood across the Widow Harding who had been positioned by a window.

"Yes, today mother," Graham replied, gazing out at the ocean. "While the sun is still shining."

The Widow Harding leaned to her side and eyed Mr. Henning, "Are you *sir*, in agreement with this foolhardy nonsense?"

Mr. Hubert Henning looked across at his daughter and soaked in her happiness. "Yes, Madam ... While the sun is still shining," he quipped, giving the Duke a wink.

The Widow Harding noticed his playfulness then asked, "Is the Reverend Carmichael in town, Your Grace?"

"If not then we shall take a trip to St. Matthews in Southwick," Graham replied, beaming into Selina's eyes.

It seemed she had been ambushed and the Widow Harding gazed around the room and rested on Lord Duncan Rowley. She looked at him up and down then straight back at Selina, "Did you tell him, dear? I am assuming you told His Grace about his son?"

Selina's smile dropped, and her heart fell to the pit of her stomach. She was going to tell him *after* their wedding, when the timing was right. She never intended the truth to be blurted out so nonchalantly, and without feeling! "No, Widow Harding, I have not."

"What?" Graham stood, confused.

"What is she talking about?" Hubert asked, walking up towards his daughter.

"What did she just say?" Martha asked Elizabeth who in turn shrugged her shoulders.

Selina then turned her head and stepped over to Duncan, grabbing his shoulders she bore into his uncertain eyes, "I never intended for you to find out this way."

Duncan opened his mouth and then latched onto her stare, "Lord Rowley is not my father?"

With her hand still on her son's shoulder, Selina gazed around at her family all with questioning eyes. The Widow Harding in the corner, nodding her head and the Duke now, in complete shock. *There was no way out, but to give in,* she thought as she looked up at her son, and then back at the Duke. "I request a private audience with His Grace and my son."

The Widow Harding stayed seated and then eyed Mr. Hubert Henning and his brother both motionless as well. The two females on the couches were not budging either, and she remarked, "Seems today is a good day for a lightening bolt, would you not agree Mr. Henning?"

Hubert turned towards his brother first and then watched him as he lifted his chin up to confirm that indeed, the Widow Harding was speaking directly at *him*. He hesitated, then voiced, "We are a close family Madam, and if my daughter has been harboring a secret for these past many years, then she did so with great hardship."

The Widow Harding nodded her head in agreement, "Consider us window dressing my dear, tell the Duke before his head bursts open with questioning."

Selina circled her eyes around the room and then over at the Duke one last time. "Seems there is no way out but to give in," she relayed, walking over to him and staring into his eyes. "I left that morning with more than shame to my character," she voiced, circling her eyes around his stunned countenance. "Lord Rowley and I married a month later, but I was still unsure that the baby was yours." She stopped and then opened her arms wide for her son to come closer, having the threesome create a circle of certainty. "Duncan's birth was a month early, and when he turned five and his hair darkened, I was convinced that he was not of *Rowley* blood, but of *Harding*."

Graham swallowed his sentiment and finally rested eyes on Duncan. A growing boy at nearly sixteen, with his same hair and eye color, even his nose was identical to his; he smiled at the young man. "I have a child," he relayed loud for everyone to hear. He gazed around the room and at all the smiling, tearful faces. Then he turned towards his mother, and happily shouted, "I have a child!"

The Widow Harding dabbed at her eyes with her handkerchief, "Yes—yes, I heard you the first time."

Graham allowed a tear to escape down his cheek, and grabbed at Selina first then opened his other arm for his son to walk into. Giving both of them a warm embrace, Graham leaned over and kissed Selina on her lips, and then lie his cheek down on Duncan's head who had been sobbing on his chest.

The Widow Harding blew her nose before blurting out, "Mr. Henning, are *you* by any chance open to courtship?"

YOU MIGHT ALSO LIKE

THE SURPRISE HEIR

In the charming era of Regency England, a tale of unexpected love and enduring destinies unfolds. **Edmund Gallagher**, a distant relative to the prestigious Lord of Langston Hall, lives a modest life far removed from the grandeur of his noble kin. His childhood memories of Langston Hall are few, but one delightful memory of climbing a treehouse with the young lord, **Rupert Hargrove**, continues to warm his heart through the years.

Now, decades later, Rupert, hailed as the dashing heir to Langston Hall, is poised to marry the impeccable Miss Abigail

Stronghold, securing his personal happiness and a prosperous future for the estate. However, just as wedding bells are to ring, an unforeseen tragedy befalls Rupert, turning Langston Hall upside down.

Equally entrapped by societal expectations and her burgeoning feelings, Miss Stronghold also finds herself at a crossroads. With the stability of Langston Hall and the future of its inhabitants uncertain, will Edmund and Abigail confront the dictates of their class and follow their hearts, or will they forsake personal happiness for the sake of tradition and duty?

This Regency romance weaves a compelling story of love, loss, and the choices that define us.

The Thunderbolt Series - Book 1

Ebook & Paperback

LOVE IN WINTER

LOVE LOST IN THE SEASON? SEARCHING FOR A WARM EMBRACE

Is Lady Alicia destined for a loveless marriage or a life on the shelf?

Follow Lady Alicia Henley's plight as societal pressures force her into the London Season. At twenty-five, she's adept at dodging suitors and yearns for something more than a preordained match.

But as the season closes and options dwindle, a drastic choice presents itself.

Will she settle for a loveless union or embark on a daring adventure across the sea?

The Caribbean beckons with the promise of sunshine and perhaps love.

Dive into a captivating tale of defying expectations and finding love in the most unexpected places.

Love in Winter is perfect for readers who adore:

- Regency Romance with a Twist
- Strong Female Leads Who Break the Mold
- Exotic Adventures that Heat Up the Pages

Escape the Ballroom and Discover Where True Love Waits!

A Regency Standalone Novella

Ebook & Paperback

ABOUT TRISHA

Hey, it's Trish...

I'm a Romance Author of 34+ books, plus an Indie Book Publisher of 48+ Pen Name Authors.

I've been writing romance with a whole lot of heat lately. I love to write fun, fast romances with witty leading ladies getting that gorgeous, sexy, yet lovable guy that doesn't take months to finish. Happily Ever After with a little bit of love angst in between. Whether you yearn for Historical or Modern, I always have a story for you!

Rejoice, Romance Reader…

For upcoming releases, book news, and other goodies, subscribe to my Newsletter!
https://mailchi.mp/567874a61a56/aab-landing-page

- instagram.com/authortrish
- amazon.com/Trisha-Fuentes/e/B002BME1MI
- facebook.com/booksbyTrish
- youtube.com/theardentartist

ALSO BY TRISHA FUENTES

✻ **Modern Romance** ✻

A Sacrifice Play

Faded Dreams

Never Say Forever

✻ **Historical** ✻

The Anzan Heir

Magnet & Steele

The Relentless Rogue

One Starry Night

In The Moonlight With You

Captivating the Captain

The Merry Widow

Unrequited Love

The Summer Romance of the Duke

❊ Series ❊

HOLLINGER

Dare To Love - Book 1

A Matchless Match - Book 2

Arrogance & Conceit - Book 3

Impropriety - Book 4

SERVICE•DAUGHTER

The Steward's Daughter - Book 1

The Cook's Daughter - Book 2

The Curator's Daughter - Book 3

THUNDERBOLT

The Surprise Heir - Book 1

A Dance of Deception - Book 2

Win the Heart of a Duchess - Book 3

OBSESSION

Unsuitable Obsession - Part One

Broken Obsession - Part Two

ESCAPE

Swept Away - Book 1

Fire & Rescue - Book 2

The Domain King - Book 3

AGE • GAP • ROMANCE

Whispers of Yesterday - Book 1

His Encore, Her Ecstasy - Book 2

Against the Wind - Book 3

www.ingramcontent.com/pod-product-compliance
Lightning Source LLC
LaVergne TN
LVHW051954060526
838201LV00059B/3635